# Molly's Family

## Nancy Garden

Pictures by Sharon Wooding

Farrar Straus Giroux • New York

"Friday is Open School Night," said Ms. Marston, Molly's kindergarten teacher. "Everyone's family is invited to come and visit. What can we do to make our room look nice?"

"We could dust and clean," said Crista.

"We could wash the windows," said Luis.

"We could build a big castle," said Danielle.

"We could draw pictures," said Molly. "And put them on the walls."

"What good ideas!" Ms. Marston said. "Let's get started."

Crista got the duster. Adam got the broom.

Luis washed the windows with Lili.

Danielle got out the blocks. Kevin and Sarah helped her build the castle.

Molly and Stephen and Tanya and Tommy got out paper and crayons.

"I'm going to draw our classroom," said Stephen.

"I'm going to draw my house," said Tanya.

"I'm going to draw our Open School Night," said Tommy.

"I'm going to draw my family," said Molly.

Molly worked very hard on her picture.

First she drew Mommy. Then she drew Mama Lu. And then she drew Sam, her puppy. Finally she put in some green grass and a big yellow sun.

"There," said Molly. "I'm done."

Tommy looked at Molly's paper. "That's not a family," he said.

"It is so!" said Molly. "It's my family."

"Where's your daddy?" asked Tommy.

"I don't have a daddy," said Molly. "I have Mommy and Mama Lu and Sam."

"You can't have a mommy and a mama," said Tommy. "Can she, Stephen?"

Stephen shook his head. "I don't think so," he said. "But you don't have to have a daddy. I don't have a daddy." He showed Molly his picture. "This is our classroom," he said. "And this is my mommy and my sister, Jackie, coming to see it."

"See?" said Tommy. "Stephen's only got one mommy. That's all you can have."

"It is not!" said Molly.

Tommy laughed. "Molly says she has a mommy and a mama," he told everyone. "But there's no such thing."

"I have a grandma and a mommy and a daddy and two brothers," Tanya said.

"I just have a daddy," said Adam. "Daddy and me!"

"And I have a daddy and a mommy," Tommy said. "No one has two mommies."

Molly tried not to cry.

"What's the matter here?" asked Ms. Marston.

"Molly says she has a mommy and a mama," said Tommy. "But you can't have a mommy and a mama. Can you?"

Ms. Marston sat down and looked at Molly's picture. "Who is this?" she asked.

Molly sniffed. "Mama Lu," she said.

"And who is this?"

"Mommy." Molly wiped her nose with a tissue Tanya gave her.

"Is Mama Lu visiting?" asked Ms. Marston.

"No."

"Is she your aunt?"

"No," said Molly. "She is my Mama Lu."

"So," said Ms. Marston, "it looks to me as if you can have a mommy and a mama."

Soon the bell rang, and Ms. Marston said it was time to go home.
Molly took her picture home on the bus.

That night at bedtime Molly asked, "Mommy, you're my real mommy, aren't you?"
"Why, yes, sweetie," said Mommy. She sounded surprised. "Of course I am!"
"Is Mama Lu my real mama?"
"Yes, Molly," said Mommy. "She is."

"But Tommy says you can't have a mommy and a mama."
Mommy hugged Molly. "Tommy doesn't know everything," she said.
Mommy called Mama Lu to come in, and told her what Tommy had said.
"Well, isn't that silly," said Mama Lu. "Look at us!"

"When Mama Lu and I were first living together," said Mommy, "we decided we had so much love that we wanted to share it with a baby."

"So your mommy had you," said Mama Lu. "She's your birth mommy. I went to a judge and told him I wanted you to be my little girl, too. He said I could adopt you. So I'm your adopted mommy."

"I bet there are other girls and boys in your school who are adopted," said Mommy.

"Do they have a mommy and a mama?" asked Molly.

"Some of them might, sugar," said Mama Lu. "There are lots of different kinds of families."

"That's right," said Mommy. "Okay, Molly?"
"I guess so," Molly answered.

But the next day Molly left her picture at home.

When she got to school, she peeked into her classroom. It looked really nice. It was very clean, and the windows sparkled. The castle was perfect. Steven's and Tanya's and Tommy's pictures were on the walls.

Ms. Marston came to the door. "Molly," she said, "where's your picture?"

"At home," said Molly.

"Why?"

"Because Tommy said you can't have a mommy and a mama. No one else does."

"But," said Ms. Marston, "you have a mommy and a mama, don't you?"

"Yes," Molly said. "I do."

"Well then," said Ms. Marston, "doesn't that mean you can have a mommy and a mama?"

Molly still wasn't sure.

"I hope you bring your picture back," said Ms. Marston. "Tomorrow is Open School Night. I'd like to hang your picture so everyone can see what a nice family you have."

Molly thought about that while she hung up her coat. She remembered what Mama Lu had said about there being different kinds of families. She looked at Stephen's picture, which showed his mommy and his sister coming to visit the kindergarten room. She remembered what Tanya said about having a grandma and a mommy and a daddy and two brothers, and what Adam said about just having a daddy. Mama Lu was right!

There even were different kinds of families in her very own class!

Molly also remembered what Mommy had said about how she and Mama Lu had so much love they wanted to share it with a baby.

"And that baby was me," Molly whispered. That made her feel warm inside.

The next day, Molly took her picture back to school.

"Here, Ms. Marston," she said.

"Oh, Molly, thank you!" said Ms. Marston. "Look, everyone. Here's Molly's nice family again." She held up Molly's picture. "Here's her mommy," she said. "Here's her Mama Lu. And here's her puppy, Sam."

"I have a puppy, too," said Tommy. "Can he come to Open School Night?"

"If he's on a leash," said Ms. Marston. "Everybody in your families can come," she said to the whole class. "All kinds of family members. And all kinds of families."

Ms. Marston hung Molly's picture on the wall, near Tommy's.

They all put away their toys and their crayons and their storybooks to finish making the room ready for Open School Night.

That evening all the families came—even Tommy's and Molly's puppies! And everyone had a wonderful time.

*For Maggie and Abby*
—*N.G.*

*For Emma*
—*S.W.*

Text copyright © 2004 by Nancy Garden
Illustrations copyright © 2004 by Sharon Wooding
All rights reserved
Distributed in Canada by Douglas & McIntyre Ltd.
Color separations by Chroma Graphics PTE Ltd.
Printed and bound in the United States of America by Phoenix Color Corporation
Designed by Barbara Grzeslo
1  3  5  7  9  10  8  6  4  2

Library of Congress Cataloging-in-Publication Data
Garden, Nancy.
    Molly's family / Nancy Garden ; pictures by Sharon Wooding.
       p.  cm.
    Summary: When Molly draws a picture of her family for Open School
Night, one of her classmates makes her feel bad because he says she
cannot have a mommy and a mama.
    ISBN 0-374-35002-7
    [1. Family—Fiction.   2. Schools—Fiction.   3. Lesbian mothers—
Fiction.]   I. Wooding, Sharon, ill.   II. Title.

PZ7.G165 Mo 2004
[E]—dc21

                                                                2002029784